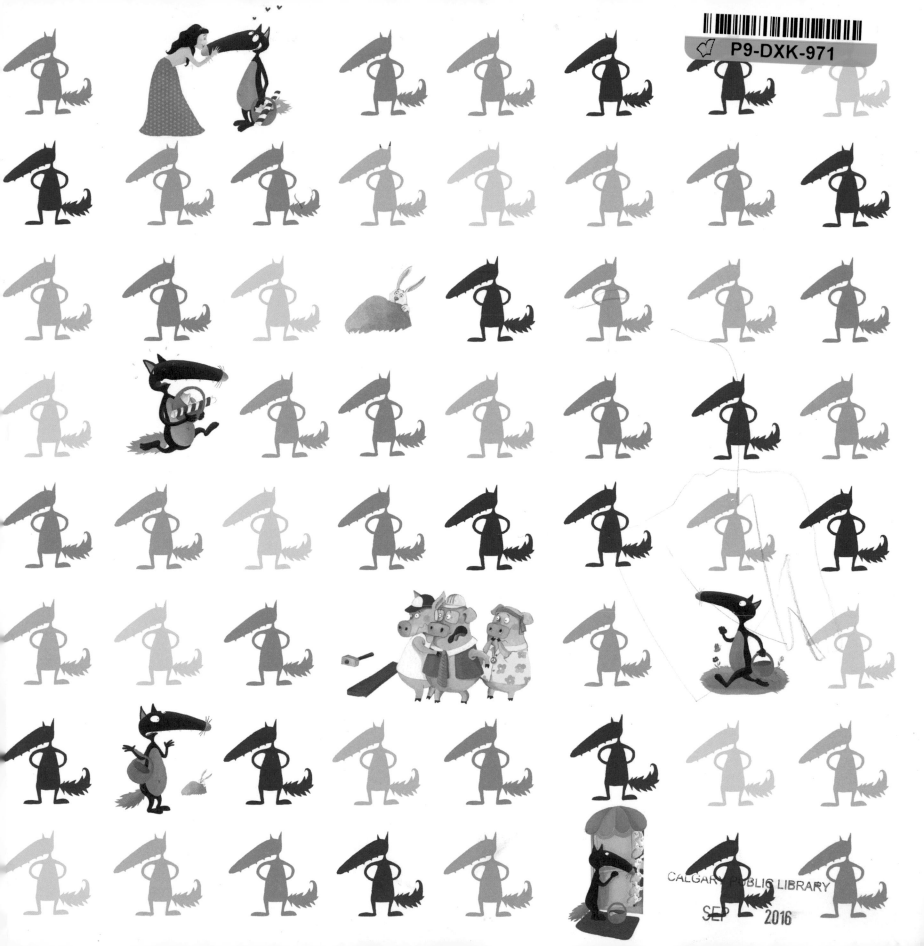

P9-DXK-971

CALGARY PUBLIC LIBRARY
SEP 2016

To Fairy Tales, past and present, from here, there and everywhere...
and to their authors who have so often delighted me...
OL

To all the little piglets, chicks, kids and other small creatures
who are still afraid of the Big Bad Wolf...
ET

The Wolf
Who Visited the Land of Fairy Tales

Text by Orianne Lallemand
Illustrations by Éléonore Thuillier

AUZOU

When the Wolf woke up that morning, the sun was shining high in the sky. The weather was perfect for the big Spring Tea Party, which was taking place that very afternoon in the forest.

"This year, I'll make an apple cake for the Tea Party," declared the Wolf.
"The only problem is I don't know how to bake."

So, he decided to go into the forest in search of someone who could help. He grabbed a basket and off he went!

The Wolf walked for hours without coming across anyone.
Finally, as he turned a bend, he came face-to-face
with three little pigs who were building their houses.

"Help!" cried the little pigs. "The Big Bad Wolf has come to gobble us up!"
"What are you talking about?" exclaimed a horrified Wolf.
"I would never gobble up cute little pigs like you."
"If you don't, then you'll huff and puff
and blow our houses down!"

"Not by a hair on my chinny-chin-chin!" swore the Wolf.
"I only want to make an apple cake, but I don't know how to bake."

The Three Little Pigs looked at each other in amazement.
"What about Aunt Rosetta's recipe?" suggested one little pig.
"Her apple cake is the best in the world!"
"Okay, but on one condition," added the wisest of the little pigs.
"He helps us finish our houses!"

The Wolf cheerfully set to work.
When he had finally finished, he was aching
all over, but at least he had Aunt Rosetta's recipe.
All he needed now were the ingredients:
flour, butter, eggs, sugar, and of course, apples.

As the Wolf continued on his way, he pictured his cake:
it would be light, soft, sweet, mmm... delicious!
His mouth was watering. "First, I need the flour," he said.
"Why don't I ask here?"

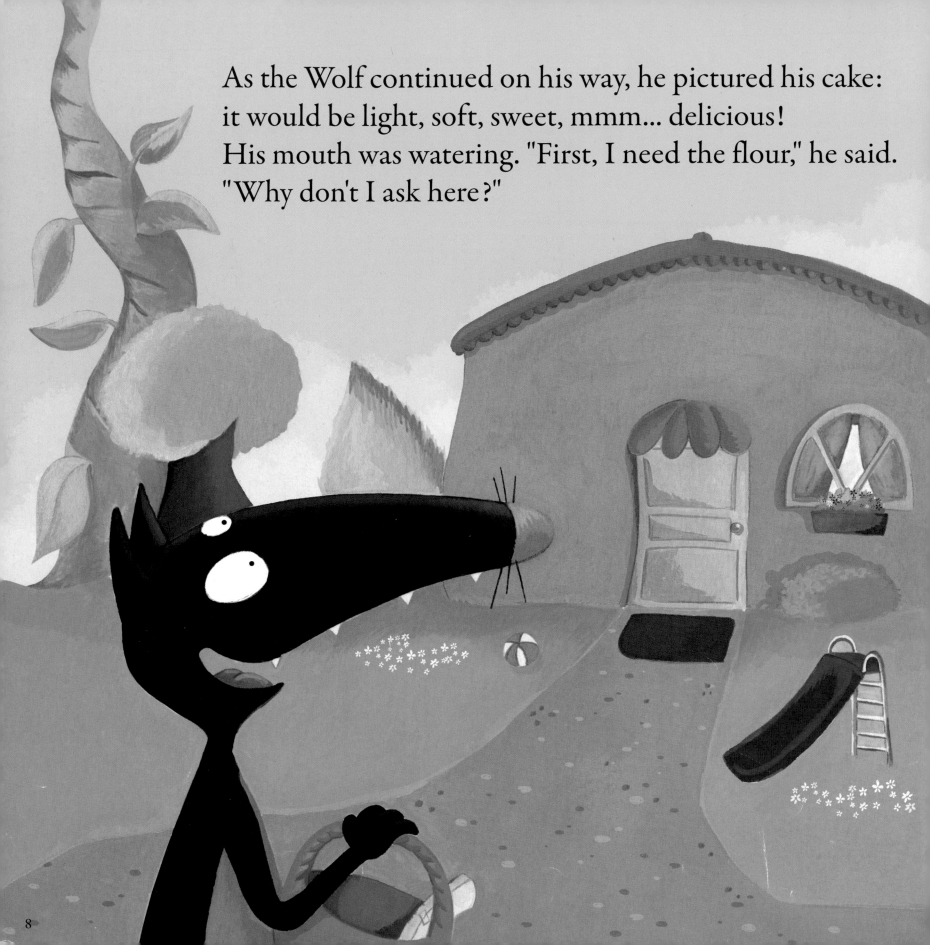

Knock, knock, knock! Slowly, the heads of seven cute kids peeped out from behind the door.

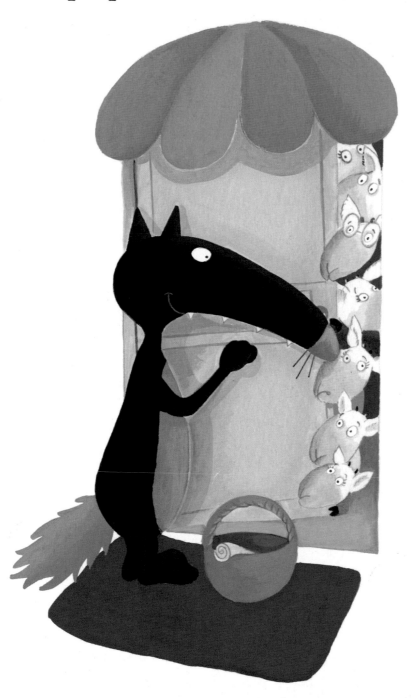

The Wolf stepped forward and... **BANG!** He was struck on the head.

When the Wolf awoke, he was tied to a chair and had a pounding headache!
"Well Mr. Wolf, you're not so cunning after all," scolded mommy goat.
"Of course not!" exclaimed the Wolf. "All I wanted was some flour."
"Flour? So you could trick your way into my house and eat my kids!"
"What? No!" stammered the Wolf. "I only need flour to make my cake."

As it turned out, mommy goat loved to bake, and in exchange for Aunt Rosetta's recipe, she gave our Wolf a bag of flour...

... and a good kick in the behind!

The Wolf continued on his way, muttering under his breath.
He had never imagined that making a cake would be so complicated.
He was still grumbling when he heard someone singing.
It was a little girl wearing a red hooded top.

"Hey!" called the little girl. "I know you... you're the Big Bad Wolf!"
The Wolf sighed... here we go again.
"Don't be afraid," he said in his softest voice. "I will not eat you."
"I know," said the little girl, shrugging her shoulders.
"You're big but you don't look that bad."

Relieved, the Wolf sat down in the grass with Little Red Riding Hood, and while they shared a piece of cake he told her about Aunt Rosetta's recipe. "If you play with me," said the girl, "I'll give you some butter for your cake."

For hours, the Wolf played tag, hide-and-seek, and kick-in-the-can.

In the end, the Wolf was tired of playing games and horsing around, but at least he now had butter in his basket.

"Now I need eggs," said the Wolf. As he looked up, he noticed a nest in a nearby tree. On his way up, he heard a scream and spotted a fox with a little red hen in his paws.

"You'll be delicious in my stew," said the fox thinking how this would please his mother. "We will relish every bite tonight!"

"Poor little hen," thought the Wolf. "I can't let her be eaten."
Without making a sound, he climbed down the tree and followed the fox.

The Wolf waited patiently for the fox to fall asleep to free the hen. "Poor little me!" she moaned. "Escaping the paws of the fox only to end up in the jaws of the Big Bad Wolf..."

"Don't worry, I'm not going to eat you," promised the Wolf.
"But we'd better hurry lest the fox wakes up."

The little red hen was so grateful, she offered to knit
the Wolf the best pair of shorts a wolf had ever seen.
"Uh, no thank you," the Wolf politely replied.
"However, I do need some eggs for my recipe."

The Wolf started off again and soon came across a spectacular house made of gingerbread, sugar, and cookies. "This is awesome!" exclaimed the Wolf. "Just when I'm looking for some sugar to bake my cake." Suddenly, a horrible witch appeared at the door.

"Champ, chomp, crunch!
Who's nibbling at my humble abode?"
she grumbled. "A wolf? Ugh!
I'm going to turn you into one fat
chicken... you'll taste better this way!"

"No way!" yelled our scared Wolf who skedaddled as fast as he could!

With the witch hot on his heels, the Wolf ran and ran until he reached a cottage, and rushed into it.

"Hello, my friend," said Snow White softly. "Who's chasing you?"
"A witch!" replied the panting Wolf. "She wants to turn me into a chicken!"
"Don't worry," said Snow White. "She won't find you here. Take a nap by the fireplace."
The Wolf gratefully sat down and fell fast asleep.

When the Wolf woke up, he told
Snow White about the Tea Party,
Aunt Rosetta's recipe and all of the
strange things that had happened
to him in the forest.

"It's because you're in the Land of Fairy Tales!" explained the girl. "By the way, here are some nice apples for your cake."

The Wolf stared suspiciously at the beautiful red apples. "The wicked Queen hasn't touched them, I promise!" said Snow White, laughing. The Wolf sighed with relief and thanked her.

Snow White then led the Wolf to her wondrous mirror and asked, "Mirror, mirror on the wall, who is the fairest wolf of all?"
"This one is the cutest one of all," replied the mirror smiling.
"The most adorable our eyes have ever seen.
Can we keep him here with us?"

"No, dear mirror," answered Snow White.
"You must send him back to his forest.
But before you do..."

Snow White placed a soft kiss on the Wolf's muzzle
and he immediately felt himself blushing, spinning,
blushing, spinning...

The Wolf woke up in a daze. He shook his head and realized he was back at home with, at his feet, the basket full to the brim. "Yippee!" he exclaimed. "I've got everything I need to make my cake. Quick! Let's bake!"

The Wolf went into his kitchen and followed Aunt Rosetta's recipe to the letter. He sliced, poured, mixed... and when he opened the oven, his apple cake was baked to perfection! Suddenly, he heard **Knock, knock, knock**! Someone was at the door.

"Hi, sweetie," said Grandma.
"We've come to fetch you for the Tea Party!"

Many of the Wolf's friends were already seated at the table,
ready to start the feast.
"Ah, here you are, at last!" exclaimed Valentino.
"What have you brought for the Tea Party?"
"Aunt Rosetta's famous apple cake and...
some new friends too," replied the Wolf.

Aunt Rosetta's Apple Cake

1 cup flour
1/2 cup semi-salted butter
1/2 cup sugar
3 fresh eggs
3 large apples
1 teaspoon of baking powder

1. Melt the butter.
2. Mix the butter and sugar with a whisk or a fork.
3. Add the beaten eggs to the mixture.
4. Gently fold in the sifted flour and baking powder.
5. Peel and cut the apples into small pieces and gently stir them into the cake batter.
6. Pour the batter into a buttered cake pan.
7. Bake at 350 °F for 40 min.

General Director: Gauthier Auzou
Senior Editor: Laura Levy
Layout: Annaïs Tassone, Eloïse Jensen
Production: Lucile Pierret
Project Manager for the present edition: Ariane Laine-Forrest
Proofreading: Rebecca Frazer
Translation from French: Susan Allen Maurin
Original title: *Le Loup qui découvrait le pays des contes*

© 2014, Editions Auzou
© 2016, Auzou Publishing for the present edition

All rights reserved. No part of this book may be used or reproduced
in any form or by any means, electronic or mechanical, including
photocopying, recording, or by any information storage and retrieval
system, without permission in writing from the Publisher.
ISBN: 978-2-7338-3923-2

Printed in China in January 2016

Who's Afraid of the Big Bad Wolf?

Meet the Wolf! His quirky, tongue-in-cheek humor and fun-loving personality is perfect for children. And his lively adventures appeal to both early readers and parents alike.

The Wolf series is now a household name in France, thanks to the fundamental concepts—such as accepting yourself, birthdays, and history—subtly woven into each story. Welcome the Wolf into your home, too!

Being naughty has never been so good!

In the same series:

  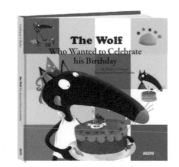

Also available:

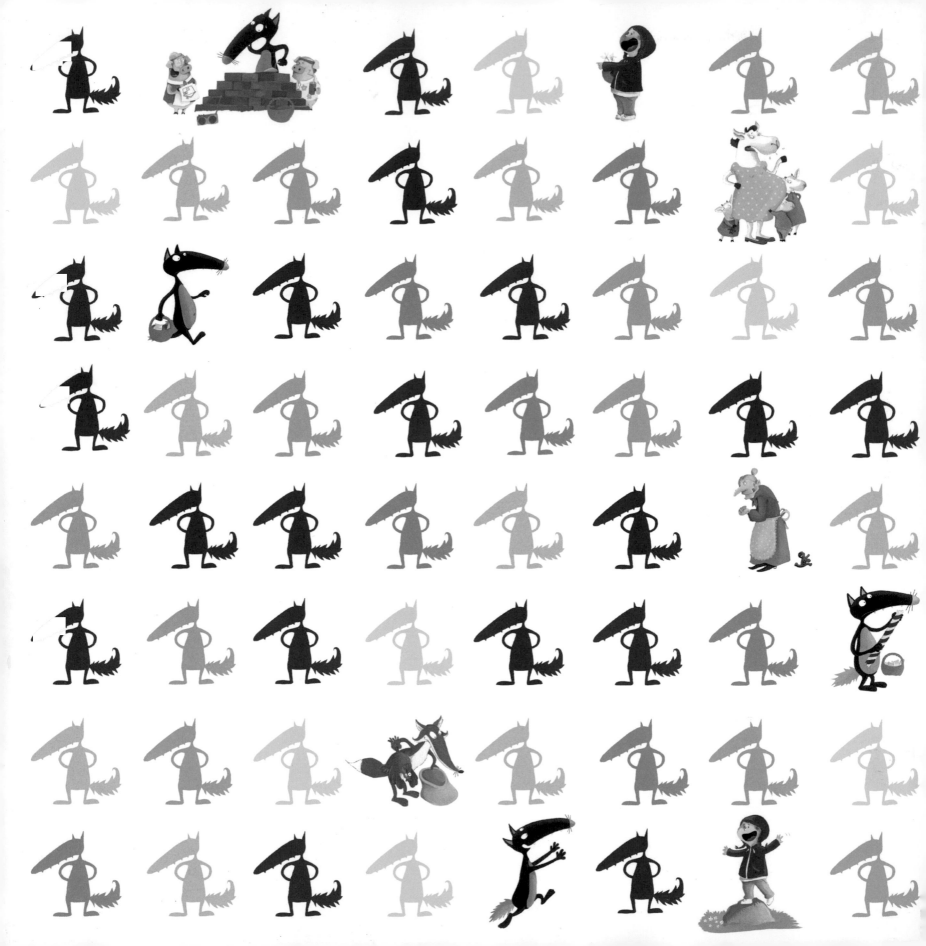